Written by Sue Graves
Illustrated by Jan Lewis
Designed by Blue Sunflower Creative

Language consultant: Betty Root

This is a P³ book
This edition published in 2004

P³
Queen Street House
4 Queen Street
Bath, BA1 1HE, UK

ISBN 1-40541-863-X
Printed in China

The Great Space Race

p^3

Notes for Parents

Reading with your child is an enjoyable and rewarding experience. These **Gold Stars** reading books encourage and support children who are learning to read.

The **Gold Stars** reading books are filled with fun stories, familiar vocabulary, and amusing pictures. Sharing these books with your child will ensure that reading is fun. It is important, at this early stage, for children to enjoy reading and succeed. Success creates confidence.

Starting to read

Start by reading the book aloud to your child, taking time to talk about the pictures. This will help your child to see that pictures often give clues about the story.

Over a period of time, try to read the same book several times so that your child becomes familiar with the story and the words and phrases. Gradually, your child will want to read the book aloud with you. It helps to run your finger under the words as you say them.

Occasionally, stop and encourage your child to continue reading aloud without you. Join in again when your child needs help. This is the next step toward helping your child become an independent reader.

Finally, your child will be ready to read alone. Listen carefully to your child and give plenty of praise. Remember to make reading an enjoyable experience.

Using your Gold Stars stickers

You can use the **Gold Stars** stickers at the back of the book as a reward for effort as well as achievement. Learning to read is an exciting challenge for every child.

Remember these four important stages:

- Read the story **to** your child.
- Read the story **with** your child.
- Encourage your child to read **to you**.
- Listen to your child read **alone**.

Spike lived on Planet Zed. He lived on
Planet Zed with his mom, dad and grandma.

Spike also had a robot called Spog.

Every day, Spike went to Space School.
He went with all the other children on
the planet. Spike liked Space School.
Mr. Moon was Spike's teacher. He showed
the children how to do lots of things.

He showed them how to float in space.

He showed them how to jump over craters.

He showed them how to turn
head over heels.

But, best of all, Mr. Moon showed the children how to fly skyrockets.

He showed them how to zoom into space.

He showed them how to zip over craters.

Loop the loop!

He even showed them how to loop the loop!
Spike liked looping the loop best of all.

One day, Spike ran home from school. He was very excited.

"We are going to have a Great Space Race next Friday," he said. "We have to build our own skyrocket. Will you help me, Dad?"

"Of course," said Dad. "But first, we must draw some plans."

Spike and Dad drew lots and lots of plans.

"Let's build this one," said Spike. "This is the best plan of all."

"Beep, beep!" said Spog.

Spike and Dad built the skyrocket. They built
it from pieces of wire and lots of tin cans.
Spog helped, too. Soon, it was ready.

16

"It's the best skyrocket on Planet Zed,"
said Spike. "Thanks, Dad."

"Now we must think of a name for it,"
said Mom.

"I think we should call it 'The Super-Looper',"
said Grandma.

"Beep, beep!" said Spog.

The next day, Spike tried out his new
Super-Looper. Spog went with him.

They zoomed into space.

They zipped over craters.

Then, they looped the loop.

"Wow!" said Spike. "It's so fast!"

Spog felt very ill.

"Be-eep! Be-eep!" he said.

Soon, it was the day of The Great Space Race. The skyrockets were in line to start the race. A boy called Dak was next to Spike.

"That's a tin can!" laughed Dak. "That will never win the race."

Spike felt very angry.

"It's not a tin can," he said. "It's the best skyrocket on Planet Zed."

"On your marks! Get set! Go!" said Mr. Moon.

The skyrockets zoomed into space. They
zipped over craters. Then, they looped the
loop. Spike and Dak were out in front.

"I can see the finish," said Spike. "I must go faster."

Just then, Dak shot past him.

"Oh, no!" said Spike. "Dak is going to win!"

Suddenly, Dak's skyrocket began to shake a little. Then, it began to shake a lot. There was a loud bang! Dak fell out and the skyrocket landed on the ground with a thump!

Spike saw Dak falling and looped under Dak. Dak landed in Spike's Super-Looper just as they crossed over the finish line.

"We've won! We've won!" said Spike.

Everyone clapped and cheered.

"You were right, Spike," said Dak. "Your skyrocket isn't a tin can at all. It's the best Super-Looper on Planet Zed."

Mr. Moon stuck a gold star on Spike's Super-Looper.

Well done!

"Well done, Spike," said Mr. Moon. "You built a very good skyrocket."

"Beep, beep!" said Spog.

Answer these questions. Look back in the
book to find the answers.

Where did
Spike live?

What was Spike's
robot called?

Who showed
Spike how to fly
a skyrocket?

What was the name of
Spike's skyrocket?

What happened
to Dak?

Who won the race?

Now retell the story in your own words.

Gold Stars

Gold Stars reading books are for children who are beginning to read.

- Familiar, repeated vocabulary
- Short sentences
- Large, clear type
- Pictures that support the text
- Review activity